THE LION WHO STOLE MY ARM

For Colleen Begg

Text copyright © 2013 by Nicola Davies
Illustrations copyright © 2013 by Annabel Wright

First U.S. edition 2014

Library of Congress Catalog Card Number 2013943082
ISBN 978-0-7636-6620-0

BVG 18 17 16 15 14 13
10 9 8 7 6 5 4 3 2 1

Printed in Berryville, VA, U.S.A.

This book was typeset in ITC Usherwood.
The illustrations were done in watercolor.

Candlewick Press
99 Dover Street
Somerville, Massachusetts 02144

visit us at www.candlewick.com

and chased fish into nets stretched between their hands, sometimes holding fish in their mouths because two hands were not enough to hold on to their nets and their catch.

"If I had a mouth as big as yours," Pedru teased Enzi, "I'd have twice as many fish."

Enzi grinned, showing just how wide his mouth could stretch. "I think I could swallow a crocodile!" he declared.

"My mouth is small," said Samuel, "and I still caught more fish than you, Pedru!"

By the time the boys had tied their fish onto sticks to carry home, the sun was already dipping behind the trees.

"We're going to have to hurry," Pedru said. The others nodded. They knew it was a long way back and it could be dark before they reached the village. Of course, they were brave boys and not afraid of the dangers of nighttime in the bush: the hippos grazing on the bank that will bite you in two if you disturb their supper; the leopards and lions

Chapter One

Pedru had been fishing with his best friends, Samuel and Samuel's big brother, Enzi. They'd chosen a spot where the river rushed over rocks and was clear enough to see fish underwater and shallow enough to keep them safe from crocodiles. They'd ridden the currents between the boulders

THE
LION WHO STOLE MY
ARM

NICOLA DAVIES

with illustrations by
ANNABEL WRIGHT

CANDLEWICK PRESS

stalking you, quieter than breath; the hyenas that will crack your bones; the crocodiles that will drag you under the water. No, what worried the boys much more was how angry their mothers would be if they were late getting back. So they hurried along the path and didn't speak until they saw the tops of the village huts over the tall grass.

"We're late," said Samuel. "I can smell the cooking fires already."

"Don't worry," Enzi replied, putting his hand on his brother's shoulder. "We've caught so many fish that Mamma will be too busy cooking to be angry."

Enzi was right. He and Samuel had caught more than thirty fish between them. Pedru looked at the fish on his stick: ten. Ten small fish were not going to keep him out of trouble for getting home late, but ten fish and a fat guinea fowl might.

Pedru stopped walking. "You go," he told his friends. "I'm going to see if my snares have caught anything."

Before the brothers had time to remind their friend that dusk is not a good time to be creeping around in the long bush on your own, Pedru was gone.

Something had gotten to the snares before him. Freshly scattered guinea-fowl feathers dotted the clearing; whatever had eaten the birds could still be close by. Pedru scanned the ground for tracks. There, framed by the crisscross of bird feet, was a single print: four oval toes arranged like petals around a central pad, with no claw marks. Cat. Big cat. *Leopard,* he told himself. *A leopard that would take the birds from the snares and slip away. Not a lion. Not a lion that might be waiting here for a bigger meal.* The hair on Pedru's neck stood on end, and his heart pounded. Run! Run! He must run away right now! He streaked through the grass and bushes, ignoring the thorns that tore at his skin. Sweating and panting, he reached the path, with the sound of voices up ahead and the smell of fires. He leaned on his knees to catch his breath, laughing a little at himself for being so scared, relieved at being safe again.

Thwack! Pedru's legs were punched from under him. His body hit the ground, and the air was knocked out of his lungs. For a moment, he didn't hear or see anything. When his eyes and ears worked again, he found he was being dragged along on his back by his outstretched right arm. He twisted around to see what could be holding him, and he looked straight into the face of a lion.

He went numb. Time slowed down. Sounds drained from the world, leaving a bowl of silence, with Pedru and the lion at the bottom of it.

Pedru stared at the lion. It was so close that even in the fading light he could see the spotted lines on its snout where its whiskers sprouted, the deep notch on its left ear, and the scraggy tufts of mane on its neck. He could smell its breath, hot and meaty, and feel where its teeth had pierced his arm and crushed the bone, although he was too afraid to feel any pain.

The lion was bumping his body back along the path, dragging him into the long grass. *As soon as it feels safe, hidden in the bush,* Pedru said to himself, *it will eat me.* Suddenly, he stopped feeling numb and started to be very angry. This lion was not going to put an end to him!

His stick, with the fish still tied to it, was gripped in his left hand. He swung it with all his strength and hit the lion hard on the head. He felt the blow strike, and when he looked at the lion, it had a cut between its ears. Pedru hit it again, and for a moment it looked right at him, its golden eyes hot like the sun. Then it snarled and ran away, and Pedru saw that it had taken his arm.

Chapter Two

P edru woke up in the hospital. Or rather, outside the hospital on the porch in the back, because all the beds inside were full. Pedru's father, Issa, was sitting beside him, fanning away the flies with an old newspaper.

"How did I get here?" Pedru asked.

His father smiled. "I put you on my back and cycled like a crazy man."

It was ten miles over dirt roads from the village to the clinic at Madune. Even for Pedru's father, the best hunter in the village, probably in all of Africa, this was quite a feat.

Issa put down the newspaper and placed his big hand on the top of Pedru's head. "Now, my son," he asked gently, "tell me, how do you feel?"

Issa had always told Pedru never to answer any question without thinking first. So Pedru thought hard about his answer. He turned his head and looked to his right. Where his arm had been was a bandaged stump, like a white stick, ending just above where the elbow had been. For a moment, Pedru's head swam and he shut his eyes. But when he opened them again, the arm was still gone. It hurt badly where the doctor had sewn up the wound the lion had left, but Pedru knew that it would stop hurting in time. The other pain, however, would not go away so easily.

"I'm scared," he told his father. "Scared that I won't be myself anymore. I'll just be the boy with one arm." Pedru tried hard not to cry and went on: "And a boy with one arm can never be strong and be a hunter like you."

Issa listened carefully, his brow a mass of creases as he took in Pedru's words. It was a few moments before he spoke. "Pedru," he said, "tell me what you can see and hear."

"The holes in the roof," Pedru answered. "Children crying. Grown-ups whispering."

"No, not here in the clinic," Issa said. "Out there." Issa pointed beyond the porch to the patch of grass and trees where the town of Madune ended and the bush began again.

Pedru propped himself up on his good arm and looked and listened. He'd always been proud of his sharp eyes and ears, and Issa had taught him to know every bird and beast in the bush. It was a comfort now to look out into the trees and sky, so lovely in the first light of day. Pedru found that his eyes snatched up every detail, like a hungry guinea fowl pecking corn.

"There are five *barbaças** in the top of that dead tree, and a flock of *zombeteiros** in the tree next to

it. There's an eagle, too, far off. Just a speck in the sky. A fish eagle, I think."

"Good!" said Issa. "Go on!"

Pedru shut his eyes and let the sounds trickle in, as clear as the first rains after the dry season: a

*__barbaças:__ a sparrow-size bird with a loud, whistling call
*__zombeteiro:__ a crow-size bird with glossy green feathers and a bright-red beak

mad, chattering, twittering sound and a low *kurru, kurru, kurru*.

"Palm swifts* and a turaco* calling," he reported. And then he heard another sound — a sweet *si si si* almost too high for human ears. "And sunbirds. Sunbirds!" Pedru smiled and opened his eyes. His father was standing beside him.

"So," Issa said, "the finest tools of the hunter, your eyes and your ears, are still working. Now, hold tight, Pedru."

Issa scooped up the ends of Pedru's sheet, like a hammock, and lifted his son high in the air.

Pedru laughed and looked down as his father held him, high and steady, with just one hand.

"Remember, Pedru," Issa said, "you do not need two arms to be strong!"

*palm swift: a small, speedy bird that swoops around the treetops catching insects
*turaco: a beautiful big bird with a purple crest and a loud, grating voice

Chapter Three

While Pedru waited for his arm to heal enough for him to go home, he tried to remember what his father had said. He whiled away the hours in the clinic by teaching himself to tie knots one-handed, and how to carry objects by clamping them between his body and his stump. But sometimes all the things he couldn't do anymore, like climb trees or go fishing, crowded in on him. That's when he thought about the lion who had stolen his arm, about its hot breath and its wicked, fiery eyes. It was his lion now, and he spoke to it fiercely in his head.

One day, lion . . . he told it. *One day soon I will come and get you.*

He was desperate to get back to the village, afraid his father might hunt the lion without him. But his arm healed fast, and in a few days he was home. Pedru wanted to pick up his spear and bedroll and set off at once to hunt his lion. But that wasn't how it turned out.

Everybody made a big fuss over him, sure. His mother, Adalia, hugged him so tightly that he thought his other arm might break. His two little sisters, Zibi and Aji, climbed all over him, asking questions until Issa told them to stop. The whole village came by to take a look at him, prodded and poked him like a goat roasting on the fire, and then talked and talked about lions, over his head. Mr. Inroga's cousin had been killed by one, just a couple of rainy seasons ago.

"He went out to chase bush pigs from his crops," Mr. Inroga said, shaking his head, "and he never came back."

Mamma Ramina had been cycling home one day and a lioness and her cub had chased her down the road.

"She was so close!" Mamma Ramina said, fanning her face at the memory of her escape. "But I pedaled too quick for her!"

Most horrible of all was Mamma Lago's story. When she was little, a lion had burst through the straw roof of her parents' hut and taken her brother. It was a long time ago now, and still Mamma Lago shed tears whenever she spoke about it.

Everyone agreed that lions were very, very bad. Leopards and hyenas would take your goats or chickens, crocodiles would take your leg, but somehow that was just a part of the way things were, like the rains and the sun. Lions were different. Lions made people afraid and angry. And now there was Pedru's lion, which might come back and take a person for its dinner. The whole village buzzed with worry.

Pedru sat still, listening, wanting all the talk to

stop. He wanted some action instead, and he hoped that he would get it when old Mr. Massingue, the village headman, came along. His voice was like dry leaves rustling in a wind, so soft that people had to lean in close to hear him.

"Issa Bubacali is our finest hunter," Mr. Massingue announced quietly. "If this lion must be killed to keep our village safe, he will be the man for the task."

Everyone nodded gravely at Pedru's father. They all knew it was a great and dangerous duty to hunt a lion.

"What is your opinion, Issa Bubacali?" Mr. Massingue went on. "Should this lion be hunted and killed?"

Pedru's heart leaped. His father would hunt the lion, and Pedru would go with him!

But Issa shook his head. "I followed the creature's tracks," he said. "They led far away from the village. They did not come back. I searched for two whole days and found no sign."

There were exclamations of relief all around, but Mr. Massingue held up his hand. "We must remain vigilant," he said. "Not even a skilled tracker such as Issa Bubacali can predict what a lion may do. But I think, for now, there is nothing to be gained from a lion hunt."

And that was that. There would be no lion hunt. Everyone knew the rains were coming and soon there would be lots of work to do in the fields. There just wasn't time to hunt a lion who had stolen the arm of an unimportant little boy.

Pedru tried to swallow his disappointment, but it stuck fast in his throat like a big lump of gristle. He went to bed without speaking to anyone. When he lay down to sleep, he pursued the lion through his dreams.

Chapter Four

The next day was the last day of the school term before the rainy-season break, and Adalia insisted that Pedru should make the most of it. So, just like always, Pedru traveled to school with Samuel and Enzi, on their family's bike. Just like always, Enzi pedaled, Samuel rode on the cargo rack, and Pedru rode on the handlebars. But it wasn't like always. Enzi didn't try to tip Pedru off when he least expected it, and Samuel didn't crack jokes. In fact, the three boys were completely silent. When other children called out to them as they passed by —

"Hey, Samuel!"

"Keep pedaling, Enzi!"

— it only made the silence worse. The sun danced through the grasses and the trees, just as it always did, but no one called out, "Hey, Pedru!"

There was a soccer game happening when the boys got to school. The ball was just a bundle of grass

wrapped in string, but the teams were still two international sides — Bafana Bafana, for South Africa, and the Black Mambas, for Mozambique. Normally, Pedru would have been called in as a forward for the Mambas, but no one called him today. He left Samuel and Enzi playing with the other boys and girls from the village and went inside. Mr. Mecula would be starting class soon anyway.

There were more than seventy children in Mr. Mecula's class, and the schoolroom was already filling up; it was such a crowd that no one could have seen if Pedru had as many arms as an octopus or none at all. All the same, Pedru felt like everyone was staring at him. He found a place squashed between a toothy girl named Esperanza on his left and a boy he'd never seen before on his right. The bell rang. The soccer players rushed in and added to the chaos. Class began.

"Today, students," Mr. Mecula announced, "is the last day of the term before the rainy-season break. I am going to give you a test on spelling and handwriting."

Pedru's heart sank. Why couldn't it have been a lesson without writing? One of those lessons when they just had to read what was on the board, or listen and answer questions in class. Pedru wanted to go on being a good student.

Mr. Mecula gave out pieces of paper and pencils, and the test began. Mr. Mecula read the first word on his list: "Vulture."

That was easy. Pedru knew how to spell the names of animals and birds best of all. But writing with his left hand was so hard. The letters came out huge and wobbly, so you couldn't really see what they were.

"Next word: hyena."

Pedru tried again, hooking his left arm around the top of the paper and trying it from another angle, but it was hopeless. Inside his head, a little voice taunted him: "One-arm boy, one-arm boy." He looked at the shapes his pencil had made on the paper. One of them looked like an animal's ear, not a letter of the alphabet. Miserably, Pedru picked up his pencil and added to the earlike squiggle so at least he would look as though he were still writing. Now it really did look like an ear: a lion's ear. Without thinking, Pedru added another ear, then the top of a head. Drawing was much easier than making finicky little letters.

Somewhere above his head, Mr. Mecula's test went on, while Pedru slowly drew: sly, slanting eyes; a dotted pattern of whiskers; a deep notch in one of the ears; the straggly beginnings of a mane. Pedru

was in a world of his own. He didn't notice that the class was empty and the children had all run out into the yard for break time until Mr. Mecula came to stand right beside him.

Pedru looked at Mr. Mecula's face and pointed to his drawing. "It's the lion who stole my arm," he said quietly, hoping that an explanation would somehow get him out of trouble.

But Mr. Mecula wasn't angry at all. He looked carefully at the drawing. "Hmm," he said thoughtfully. He took an exercise book out of his desk drawer and gave it to Pedru. "Drawing will help you practice pen control, Pedru, so you will learn to write with your left hand. I want you to fill this exercise book with drawings and show it to me when school starts again after the rains."

Pedru flicked through the empty pages in wonder. No one ever had a whole exercise book to themselves—not ever! It was amazing, but also daunting. "Do I have to fill all the pages, Mr. Mecula?" Pedru asked.

"Yes, Pedru. You do. But I think you'll find it easier than you expect," Mr. Mecula said, pointing to the picture of the lion. "Your left hand seems to know what it's doing already!"

Chapter Five

Now that the rains had come, it was the busiest time in the fields. Everyone from the village was out working from dawn to dusk. Pedru was determined to prove himself to be just as strong and useful as always, digging, hoeing, and planting with his left hand.

"You will be like my uncle Dano," Adalia told him. "He was a fine fisherman even though a crocodile took his leg."

Pedru knew she was trying to be kind, but he didn't want to be like anyone who was a cripple. He couldn't stand how the other children looked at him now, so instead of playing soccer in his spare time, he went off on his own and practiced with his spear. He threw it over and over again, strengthening his left arm and improving his aim.

Adalia didn't let him forget Mr. Mecula's exercise book. Every evening when she lit the lamp in their hut, she put the book down in front of him. "Throwing spears isn't the only kind of practice you need!" she told him. "One drawing every day, please."

But after a few days, Adalia didn't need to nag him. It was comforting to recall some part of each day and see it come to life again under his hand. Slowly the pages began to fill up: a guinea fowl, a hammerkop,* the new shoots showing in rows in the fields, a basking lizard, his sisters carrying a bucket between them.

He stuck the drawing of the lion in the front of the book and looked at it each night. Although everyone else seemed to have forgotten his lion, Pedru would not.

The rains fell and fell. The river grew fat and spread out over the flatlands, leaving little sprigs of islands dotted

---

*hammerkop: a type of stork with a feathery crest that makes its head look like a hammer

in the muddy waters. Plants sprouted everywhere — grass, reeds, leaves, and flowers, growing green and lush where the ground had been as dry and hard as stone before the rains came. The crops in the fields sprang up, and everyone began to hope for a good harvest, with plenty to eat for the rest of the year.

But as the crops grew, bush pigs came at night to eat them, trampling the new shoots and pushing their snouts deep into the soil to eat the roots. Their long noses and pointed ear tufts began to appear most days in Pedru's exercise book. So every evening Issa and Pedru left Adalia and the girls in the village and went to the fields, to light a fire and be ready to chase the pigs out of their crops.

Pedru's family's fields were on a slope, so Pedru could look out and see the fires on other *marashambas** dotted around the land. Sounds carried in the still dark: familiar voices, tree frogs and night birds, hippos arguing down on the river. It was exciting to be out in the dark with his father, under the stars, with just a little straw lean-to to keep off

*marashamba: a plot of land where food is grown

any passing showers. It was thrilling to hear the snorts and crashes of the pigs in the field and to run toward them, shouting and waving a burning branch. But it was dangerous, too. Leopards and lions liked to eat bush pigs, and they would follow their favorite meal into the fields. Pedru thought of Mr. Inroga's cousin, eaten by a lion as he chased pigs from his crops. So when he rushed out into the dark with Issa, Pedru made himself brave by imagining throwing his spear.

I'm ready for you, lion, he told himself. *I'm ready!*

But when a lion came, Pedru wasn't ready at all. He was asleep.

A scream woke him. It filled the air — a terrible sound of pain and fear. The fire was out, and clouds covered the stars so that it was deeply dark. Pedru leaped up, calling for his father, but he was alone in the lean-to. In the blackness, he scrambled for his spear and only succeeded in tripping over the last of the fire and burning his foot. The screaming stopped, leaving an awful moment of silence before other frightened voices began calling out. Pedru's hand found a stick meant for the fire, and he ran with it toward the voices, down the hill, where the trail curved around the edge of the fields.

People were crashing through a tangle of bushes and head-high grass, their burning torches flashing through the leaves and branches. Pedru and the torchbearers broke through a last screen of greenery to see dim figures — human and lion — half hidden in vegetation and darkness. Through the flicker of shadows and his own fear, Pedru saw a spear fly; it missed, and the cat snarled and streaked away like a smear of lesser shadow, leaving a human figure quite still on the ground. Pedru stared in horror as the torchlight drew around it: a man, his father's size and build, but as broken as a stem of grass, quite dead. Pedru felt his knees give way. *No,* he thought. *No, no, no.*

Chapter Six

The next morning at dawn, Adalia was poking the fire with a stick as if she were stabbing something to death.

"He passed out chasing after that murdering beast and now you're taking him to hunt it?" she shouted. "Are you crazy?"

For once her scolding did no good. Issa stood his ground.

"Pedru fainted in shock," he told her quietly. "He thought that I was the one the lion had killed. Pedru needs to hunt this lion. He's coming with me."

It was almost the longest speech Pedru had ever heard Issa make in response to one of Adalia's attacks. He jumped away from the doorway of the hut to hide the fact that he had been eavesdropping, and he pretended to play with his little sisters, who were making a little village of stones and sticks in the mud.

"Ready, Pedru?" his father called.

Ready? Ready? Pedru had been waiting with his spear and his bedroll for half the night. If he had to wait any longer, he was afraid he might just explode with excitement and pride. As they walked through the village in the slanting early light, people came out to wish them luck. Enzi and Samuel and some of the other boys ran after Pedru and slapped him on the back, and girls looked at him from under their eyelashes. He felt like a hero already.

The tracks where Mori Pelembe had been killed by the lion had been trampled away by human feet, but beyond the little marsh, they found some clear prints in the soft ground. Pedru touched one of the paw prints with his fingers. His lion had stood right here, in this space where Pedru himself now stood. Only a few short hours separated them.

I'm coming, Pedru whispered in his head to the lion. *I'm coming to get you!*

The plan was to track the lion, then use the dead goat they had brought with them as bait, to tempt it to come within range of their spears as they lay in wait.

They followed the tracks through tall grasses and under acacia* trees all day, then camped out, taking turns to keep watch in the darkness, and set off again at dawn.

Early on the second day, they found tracks dug deep into the mud at the edge of a pond. The tracks led up, away from the band of acacias and baobabs,* onto a long slope littered with rocks. The ground was too hard here to take the imprint of a paw, but Issa found other little signs — a tiny wisp of fur caught on a spider's web, a sharp smell of cat when he put his nose close to a rock.

Then late in the morning, it rained — a downpour like buckets being tipped one after another from the purple clouds. It didn't last, but it was enough to wash away every trace of the lion's journey.

"We'll lay a scent trail with the bait, from the place where I last found a good track — the top of this ridge," Issa said. "You stay here. It's better if

*acacia: a tree with tiny delicate leaves and thorny branches
*baobab: a tree that is sometimes called the upside-down tree because of its thick trunk and mass of wiggly rootlike branches

there is as little human scent as possible."

The dead goat had gotten smelly. It oozed. Pedru watched Issa let the stinky liquid trickle over the rocks as he dragged the dead animal down the slope, through the first bit of scrubby woodland, and back to the foot of a tree.

"We'll climb up the tree and wait," said Issa.

Pedru looked up to where the trunk divided into smooth gray branches: high enough to keep them safe, but not too high for their spears to hit the lion down below. With two arms, Pedru could have climbed up there in moments. Now Issa would have to haul him up on a rope. Issa would not complain, but Pedru's heart stung.

It took some time to get the rope around one of the branches, then around Pedru's waist. But once Pedru was in the tree, he felt more useful. Issa tied the rest of their gear to the rope, and Pedru hauled it up, pulling with his left arm and looping the slack away with his stump. Then Issa spread as much goat scent around as possible and staked the goat firmly to the ground, so that the lion couldn't just grab it and run before they had a chance to throw their spears.

The preparations took all afternoon, and the sun was sinking as Issa pulled himself up into the fork of the tree beside Pedru.

"Now," Issa said, "we wait."

Pedru drew the shadows growing long across the clearing in his exercise book, but soon the darkness spread and enveloped him. As he sat in silence beside his father, Pedru had to admit that inside the excitement and the pride he'd felt all day was fear.

Chapter Seven

Every insect in Africa seemed to be crawling over Pedru's skin, especially on his left arm, where he couldn't squish them. He knew he had to sit as still and quiet as his father, but it was very hard. Pedru had never known before how long the night was when you stayed awake for all of it. By the time the crescent moon had floated halfway up the sky, he felt as though he had been awake for a hundred years.

A tiny scratching sound came from higher up the tree. Very slowly, Pedru tilted his head to look up at it and saw two bush babies* silhouetted against the sky. They leaped along the branch together, holding up their arms as if celebrating each jump. Pedru forgot all about the insects tormenting him.

Issa's elbow nudged him in the ribs, and he looked down. Moonlight streaked the space beneath their tree, with the dead goat a dark stain at its center. Something was creeping toward it, down

*bush baby: a nocturnal squirrel-size relative of monkeys, with huge eyes and ears and long back legs for leaping

the slope from the rocks above. A pale shape in the moonlight, a creature that seemed to be made of liquid, flowed between the trees and bushes, disappearing and appearing. Finally it stood still, and its eyes glowed as they reflected the moonlight. A lion's eyes!

Pedru's skin prickled, and he spoke in his head to the lion to make himself feel brave: *Come closer. Come to my spear!*

If Issa and Pedru had been still before, now they sat like stones, hardly breathing. Their eyes reached into the black-and-white world of the moonlight, out to where the lion stood at the edge of the clearing. Its glowing eyes scanned the night so that father and son wished themselves sunk into the smooth bark of the tree.

Above Pedru's head, the bush babies broke into a family squabble. They squeaked and chittered and rustled the leaves with their wild jumping. Pedru sensed the tension in his father's body draw even tighter as the lion stirred, and it turned its face

toward the tree. Pedru felt the attention of its eyes, its ears, its nose, and even its whiskers, searching the air between them.

Bush babies, the lion concluded. *Just bush babies!* Reassured now, it moved, low but swift and decisive, to the dark patch that was the goat, and it began to tear at it with its mouth and paws.

Pedru's left hand tightened on his spear, and he knew without looking that his father's right hand had done the same. But still they waited.

The lion found that it couldn't carry off the goat. It was stuck somehow. But now the lion was too hungry and irritated to be suspicious, and it pulled at the bait again, ripping off bits of flesh, no longer noticing the bush babies rustling in the trees above.

Pedru saw the spear in the lion's side before he knew that his father had thrown it. It stuck out, firmly lodged between the ribs. The lion staggered and snarled — a sound that ripped a hole in the stillness. Pedru aimed and threw with all his strength. He almost seemed to feel the spear strike home, piercing the lion's other side. Darkness flowed down the bright coat, as if the night itself were bleeding from it. The lion fell, crawled a little way, then lay still.

Pedru stared at the spears. *My spear,* he said to himself. *Thrown with my left hand! I've killed the lion who stole my arm!*

But when they climbed down to look at the body, Pedru's feeling of triumph leaked away a little. Was this his lion? He could not be sure, and without certainty he could not feel triumphant. This lion was a female, a lioness, without the scrappy start of a mane that he remembered on his lion. And he was pretty sure that his lion had not had anything around its neck. The sad, dead body at his feet was wearing a collar.

Chapter Eight

Pedru fetched help from the village, and at dusk on the fourth day, Issa and three other men carried the lioness into the space between the huts. Everyone came out to look at the body, but some didn't want to get close, as if they feared the animal could come to life. Children and women touched the fur with one finger. Some giggled nervously; some snatched their hands away in disgust. The men pushed back the lioness's lips to look at its huge stabbing teeth, and then they popped the claws out of their sheaths. Mamma Lago hit the body with a stick, then ran back to her hut crying.

But the thing that made everyone talk and ask questions, more than the beast's teeth, claws, or size, was its collar. It was a thick leather collar with a kind of plastic capsule attached to it, and a message was written in worn letters: PLEASE RETURN THIS RADIO COLLAR TO THE LION RESEARCH UNIT AT MADUNE.

Issa explained that the collar had been put on

the lion by some foreigners who lived in a compound outside Madune. The capsule on the collar sent out a signal, like the radio station that sent the news and soccer matches to the crackly old radio in Mr. Massingue's hut, and the foreigners could use the signal to tell what the lion was doing. But this explanation just made people ask even more questions.

"If they could tell where the lions were, why didn't they just kill them?"

"If they could tell what the lions were doing, why didn't they keep them from doing bad things?"

Mr. Massingue held up his hand for quiet. "I also have heard," he said, "that the foreigners sometimes help those who bring back their lion collars. They have powerful medicines and a big Land Rover that can take people to the hospital if they are very sick. I think it would be a good thing for someone from this village to take back the collar."

"I'll do it!" Pedru said. "I'll go tomorrow."

Perhaps the lion people would tell him for sure if the lioness they had speared was his lion or not.

* * *

The lion people's compound was a long ride out of
Madune. Pedru was glad to get off his father's bike
and lean it against the sign that said:

MADUNE
Carnivore
Research Station

There were two thatched huts and several tents.
A battered-looking Land Rover was parked under
a tree, and a white man with a bushy beard and

a woman with dark hair tied in an untidy bun were peering into the engine under the lifted hood. A tall young man, looking a bit like an older version of Pedru himself, sat in the shade with a laptop computer glowing on his knees. None of them noticed Pedru.

Mr. Massingue and his father had told Pedru that the lion people would be pleased to get the collar. But now that he was here, seeing the huts and tents, the car and the computer, all devoted to finding out about lions, Pedru wondered how pleased they would be about a dead lion. For a moment, he thought about leaving the collar and just running off, but then he might never know if he had speared his lion. He decided to be brave. He stepped in front of the young man with the laptop.

"Hello. I'm Pedru," said Pedru, "and I have a collar for you."

The young man was named Renaldo, and his two workmates were Beth and John. Beth was from Cape Town, and John was from New York, in

America. They were sad that the lion was dead, they said, but they were all very pleased that Pedru had brought them the collar. They thanked him, several times. They made him sit in the shade and brought him a drink of water and some cookies; they were very kind.

"The lion was speared near my village," Pedru explained cautiously. "It killed a man named Mr. Mori Pelembe. I saw it running away."

The three lion researchers nodded sadly.

"We're very sorry to hear that," said John.

"But I would like to know," Pedru went on, holding up his stump, "if it was the same lion who stole my arm."

The three researchers looked at Pedru's missing right arm, as if noticing it for the first time. For a moment, everyone was very quiet, and then John said, "Well, this collar may just be able to answer your question."

Chapter Nine

Inside the hut, Renaldo connected the collar to another computer. He explained to Pedru that it carried a record of everywhere the lion had been.* While they waited for the collar to download its story onto the laptop, Beth showed Pedru some photographs of lions on another computer screen.

*radio and satellite collars send out signals so researchers can track the animals wearing them. Signals from radio collars travel a few miles and are picked up by a radio receiver in real time.

Each lion had a name beside its picture and a little drawing of its face.

"This is how we identify lions," Beth explained. "From photos and these drawings. We tell one lion from another by their whisker spots, their ears and scars, and the size and color of their manes."

"And the color of their noses," John added, "tells us how old they are. The pinker the nose, the younger the lion; the blacker the nose, the older!"

"We give all the lions we study names," Beth said, and then she added in a pretend whisper, "because it's easier than numbers for John's old brain to remember!"

"Thanks, Beth!" John grinned. He pointed to one particular photo up on the screen. "That's Puna—the lioness this collar belonged to."

John brought up a photograph of Puna lazing in the shade of an acacia with four tiny cubs. Pedru had only ever seen lions slinking like evil spirits through the grass or snarling and spitting when a hunter had cornered them. Or dead. He had never

Signals from satellite collars go up to a satellite when it passes overhead, and they are picked up by researchers every few hours or days.

seen a lioness with cubs; he hadn't realized that lion cubs could be so tiny and so helpless, all eyes and fluffy yellow fur. Pedru had feared and hated lions all his life, but he was disconcerted to find that Puna and her cubs reminded him of his mother and his little sisters.

"The cubs were Cheli and Seti — two girls — and two boys, Samir and Anjani," Beth said, pointing to each cub on the screen. "Here's the last photo we have of them, about a year ago, when the cubs were almost grown."

Beth clicked on a photo of Puna and her cubs, now more than half their mom's size.

"Not long after that, we found Puna's two sisters speared by hunters, and Puna just disappeared," John explained.

"We guessed that something bad had happened to her and her cubs," Beth said sadly.

Not as bad as what happened to Mr. Pelembe, Pedru thought.

At last, the collar was ready to tell its story.

A map with colored dots appeared on Renaldo's screen, and they all gathered around.

"There's your village, right?" John said, pointing to a black dot on the map with the name of Pedru's village written beside it. "The orange dots show where Puna went, and the numbers beside them are the dates, OK? Can you see on this map where the attacks happened, Pedru?"

It took a moment to figure out what the map showed, and then Pedru had it! There was his village, with the trail to the river and the fields to the north, and there was the little marsh at the bend in the path. Pedru put his finger on the screen. "There is where Mr. Pelembe was killed, five days ago, and there is where the lion attacked me, before the rains."

There were orange dots all around the village.

"Hmm," said John, peering at the screen, "looks like Puna could have killed Mr. Pelembe." He pointed to a dot right next to the village. "See the date? Six days ago, right before the attack."

"She must have followed a bush pig into the marashamba," said Beth, "and when Mr. Pelembe chased the pig, he ran into her." Beth shook her head. "We've seen that happen so many times."

"But look at the dates on these dots," Renaldo said, pointing to a string of dots at the top of the screen. "This is where she was at the start of the rains: ten miles north. She didn't move south until ten days ago."

"So Puna couldn't have taken my arm," Pedru said.

"No," said Beth, "but that means the lion that did is still out there and could be a threat to your village."

John turned from the screen and looked at Pedru. "Don't suppose you got a good look at your lion, did you?" he asked.

The drawing! Why hadn't he thought of it the moment he'd seen the lion ID pictures?

"Yes!" Pedru exclaimed. "Yes, I did!"

He pulled his exercise book from his bag and

opened it to the page where he had pasted the drawing of his lion. "I drew it," he said, "but it's not very good."

John snatched the picture from Pedru's hands. "What do you mean, it's not very good?" he said. "It's a perfect ID sketch!"

Excitedly, Beth rushed to the other computer. "Pedru, you're a genius!" she said. "Take a look at this, guys."

Beth had clicked a photo of a young lion onto the screen, and John held Pedru's sketch beside it.

"Well, I'll be . . . !" said John.

"It's definitely the same animal," Renaldo added. "The whisker spots match — and the notch in the ear!"

"Absolutely!" said Beth.

John grew serious. "OK, Pedru," he said. "This is the lion that attacked you."

Pedru stared at the screen. The lion looked exactly how he remembered it. He shivered as he thought of its teeth grinding on his bone, and, in his head, he told it again, *I am coming to get you, lion!*

But now it wasn't just "lion." It had a name. It was one of Puna's cubs: Anjani.

Chapter Ten

The researchers decided to go talk to the elders of Pedru's village about the lion attacks. They put Pedru's bike on the roof of the Land Rover, and some food and camping gear in the back, and set off.

The journey was slow. The road from Madune was close to the edge of the swollen river, and the flood had washed huge holes and ruts into it. The Land Rover kept getting stuck. Pedru helped

John and Renaldo push it out of the mud while Beth drove. Pedru enjoyed feeling like part of their team, and after an hour or so of struggling together with the Land Rover, he felt comfortable enough to ask them questions.

"Why do you and Beth and John study lions?" he asked Renaldo as the Land Rover's wheels spun in yet another muddy pothole.

Renaldo put his back to the Land Rover's bumper and shoved. "There are lots of reasons," he said, "but the biggest one is that knowing what lions do helps to keep people safe from them."

Pedru dug his heels into the mud and heaved. "But why not just hunt them all and kill them? And then people would always be safe."

"Because," said John, "without lions to kill them, you'd have way more bush pigs after your crops."

"And," said Renaldo, screwing up his eyes to push even harder, "one day soon, lions will bring tourists, and tourists will bring money. Lions could give our country so much."

"Anyway," said John, looking sideways into Pedru's face, "I don't think you really want to kill lions, do you, Pedru?"

Just then, the Land Rover shot forward, dropping them all into the mud. Pedru was glad, because it meant that he didn't have to answer John's question. He wasn't sure what to say.

The shadows were growing long by the time they reached the village, and everyone came out to see who the visitors were. No one could remember the last time a car had come to their village.

Pedru felt very important as he stepped out of the Land Rover and introduced the lion researchers to Mr. Massingue and to Issa and Adalia. Beth asked him to watch over the Land Rover, while she, John, and Renaldo talked to the village elders.

Pedru was a bit put out that he was not going to be included, but being allowed to sit in the driver's seat, scolding any child who tried to climb onto the vehicle, soon made him feel better. He leaned out the window to explain to Enzi and Samuel, Adalia and his little sisters, all about ID pictures, whisker spots, radio collars, and how his drawing had identified the lion who stole his arm.

It grew dark. Still the grown-ups talked. Pedru fell asleep leaning on the steering wheel, and he woke up to the sound of his father's voice. "Pedru, wake up," Issa said. "Get ready. We're going on a lion hunt."

Pedru grabbed his bedroll and his spear from the hut. When he came out again, Issa, John, Renaldo, and Beth were leaning over a map spread on the hood of the Land Rover.

"So," John said, turning to Issa, "after it attacked Pedru, the lion headed west?"

"For six miles. I tracked it and it didn't stop," Issa told them.

"You must taste very bad," Renaldo said to Pedru.

"Pedru hit this lion hard on the head," Issa told them proudly.

"You stood up to the lion that was chewing on your arm?" said Beth.

John shook his head. "You are something else, Pedru," he said.

"Where did you find the last tracks, Issa?" Beth asked.

"Here," Issa said. "But that was before the rains. He could have gone a long, long way since then."

"Well," said Beth thoughtfully, "Anjani won't go east to his mother's old territory."

"And the land to the south is flooded from the rains," Issa added, "and the north is rocky, with not much to eat."

"So, west is where we start to look," said John. "OK, let's get going. Operation Find Pedru's Lion!"

The Land Rover bumped slowly through the grass-land and sparse trees, heading west to where Issa had last found any sign of Anjani. Every so often, they stopped to look for tracks or to climb a rock or hilltop to scan for lions sleeping in the shade of trees on the horizon.

Issa told Pedru that the plan the villagers and researchers had agreed on was to put a radio collar on Anjani, not to kill him.

"Renaldo will use the collar to check where the lion goes, and if it comes toward the village, he will warn us," Issa said.

"It's a big opportunity for us," Renaldo explained, "to study a lion we know has been a problem in the past."

"Yeah," John said. "We want to see if they can be reformed. But I think you already reformed Anjani when you hit his head, Pedru."

Pedru didn't smile.

In return for the risk of leaving the lion alive, the researchers were going to help the village to keep safe from lion attacks in the future.

"We will help build shelters and fences that can keep people and animals safe from lions," Beth said.

Pedru listened in silence. *What do I get in return*

for my arm, he thought, *if the lion who stole it goes without punishment?*

Beth leaned around as she drew the Land Rover to a stop. "Are you OK, Pedru?"

Pedru nodded, but inside, he told his lion, *I'm getting closer. And my spear is here, under my seat, lion!*

Chapter Eleven

They searched all day without seeing so much as a single paw print—only a few waterbuck* and some birds. That night they camped, cooked canned food over the fire, and talked. The researchers and Issa swapped stories about wildlife and the bush.

Pedru half listened, half slept. He heard Beth say that she had raised an orphan lion cub when she was ten and John say that he was an expert at shooting lions with a tranquilizer gun. He thought he heard Issa say that he'd been chased by a herd of crocodiles. He thought he heard that Renaldo's cousin was a rich soccer player who was going to build a safari lodge at Madune. "So people from the city can come and see lions," Pedru thought he remembered Renaldo saying.

But when Issa lay down in the tent next to him and Pedru asked sleepily if crocodiles ever chased people in herds, Issa just laughed, so Pedru knew he

*waterbuck: a large antelope found in grassland all over southern Africa

must have dreamed about Renaldo's brother, too.

The next morning, they struck camp before dawn, everyone quietly doing what needed to be done. Already, they were a team.

"That John, he is a good man," Issa told his son as they took down their tent. "He knows almost as much about the bush as I do."

As he put the tent onto the roof of the vehicle, John told Pedru quietly, "I wish I had half of your dad's tracking skill. And you're no slouch yourself."

Pedru smiled, but inside he felt bad. He liked John and Beth and Renaldo so much, but would they like him if they knew how he felt about his lion?

Pedru had the best eyes, so he was put on lookout, clinging to the roof of the Land Rover.

"Vultures!" he yelled when they were too faint and far for anyone else to see. Everyone knew that vultures could mean a lion kill.

"That way!" Pedru directed Beth. She drove as fast as she dared — sliding, skidding, bumping.

"Beth could have been a race-car driver in another life," John said as she swerved to avoid a tree stump.

The vultures were closer now. Everyone could see them, as well as a dark clump of animals on the ground below. Beth parked the Land Rover in the shade of a tree, and everyone got out quietly and climbed onto the roof with Pedru.

"Take a look, Issa," John said, handing Issa his binoculars. Pedru squinted into the light, impatient

to make out what was going on under the spiraling wheel of vultures.

"Here," said Beth. "Have mine. I need to take pictures anyway."

Over the last day or so, Pedru had had some practice with binoculars, but he still spent the first few moments getting spider images of his own eyelashes. There! Now he had it. The thrill of being able to see faraway things so clearly made his heart race with excitement.

Lions! Two of them. Young males with growing manes. They had killed a young waterbuck, probably just before dawn, but were now having to defend their kill from a crowd of hyenas. The two lions snarled and spat in fury, and the hyenas heckled and snapped, getting closer and closer.

"They will lose their kill," Issa said, handing the binoculars back to John.

"Yeah!" John grinned. "That's what I'm betting on — two hungry youngsters who missed out on breakfast."

Pedru steadied his hands and looked more closely at the lions. The smaller one, the one with the darker mane, had a notch in its left ear. Pedru felt his gaze traveling down the binoculars and out into the morning air.

You don't know it, he told his lion, *but I've caught up with you at last.*

Chapter Twelve

Pedru watched as the hyenas stripped the waterbuck's body and cracked its bones for the marrow. There was hardly anything left for the horde of hopping, squabbling vultures. The two lions skulked off and lay in the shade of an acacia a few hundred yards away, just visible through the heat haze with binoculars. The day was still, with no breeze to carry the scent of humans and make the lions wary. With all hope of recovering their kill gone, and no hunting to be done until nightfall, the lions slept. Pedru climbed down from the roof of the Land Rover to join Issa and the researchers, who were quietly planning their attack.

Beth had plugged her camera into Renaldo's laptop so they could look at her photos of the two young lions and compare them with the ID pictures. Even though the shots were taken from so far away, everyone agreed that the young lions were Puna's two male cubs, Samir and Anjani.

"So all we need to do now," said John, "is get close enough to get a tranquilizer dart into Anjani, and his brother too, if we can."

"How close must you be?" Issa asked John.

"You are speaking to the lion-darting champion of all of Africa here," John said with a mock swagger, "but all the same, I need to be quite close to be sure of a good shot. Twenty-five, maybe thirty yards?"

"Good—not as close as I thought," said Issa. "They are very hungry, these lions. We can get them close if we have bait to tempt them."

"How about this?" Renaldo grinned, holding up a small, dead goat. "I got him out of the freezer just before we left our compound. He's thawed out now."

"Mmmm, and getting smelly, too!" said Beth. "Perfect. Where should we put him, Issa?"

Before Issa could answer, Pedru spoke up. He pointed to a short line of trees, beyond the acacia where the two lions slept.

"Those waterberry trees," Pedru said. "There will be water there, and the lions will be thirsty."

Issa nodded and smiled. "That is thinking like a hunter, Pedru. Very good."

The plan was that Issa and John would wait in the trees by the goat, each with a tranquilizer gun. Although Issa didn't own a gun, he had used one many times and was a crack shot. With two guns, their chances of getting a dart into Anjani, or even darting both lions, were much greater.

"We'll use this, too," John said, pulling a small plastic recording device from the back of the Land Rover. "It'll play the sound of a bush pig squealing. The lions won't be able to resist."

When the lions were tranquilized, John would call Beth and Renaldo to bring the collars from the Land Rover.

"You will wait with them. It's too dangerous for you to come with us," Issa told Pedru. "I don't trust these dart things," he added in a whisper.

Pedru had no intention of being left out of the hunt, even if it meant disobeying Issa, so he didn't bother to argue. About an hour before dusk, as John and Issa were about to make their way to the waterberry grove with the dead goat, Pedru slipped his hand into John's pack, took out the recorder, and hid it in his tent. He said good-bye to Issa and John and wished them luck. Then he waited.

The sun sank and touched the horizon. By now John and Issa would be at the grove — too far away to come back to fetch the recorder.

"They've left the recorder behind!" Pedru told Beth and Renaldo. "I'll take it to them. Don't worry. I'll take my spear, too."

He was gone before they could say a word.

The goat was already strung up on a branch, and John and Issa were about to climb to their positions when Pedru arrived at the waterberry trees.

"Thanks a million, Pedru," said John, looking very pleased. He set the little plastic speaker at the bottom of the goat tree. "Don't know how I left it behind."

"I think I know," said Issa quietly, giving Pedru a hard look. They both knew it was too late now for Pedru to return to the camp alone.

"Can you get up into that tree?" Issa asked.

Pedru nodded. The tree had several trunks growing close together, so by bracing his feet on one and his back on another, he could work his way upward, holding his spear in his one good hand. Pedru was glad there was no time for more questions.

John turned on the playback device, and the sound of squealing bush pig filled the space under the trees and echoed out into the falling darkness.

Chapter Thirteen

T he horrible squealing and the smelly goat together worked like a charm. It wasn't even fully dark when the two lions skirted the edge of the marsh — probably getting a drink on the way — and almost bounded into the waterberry grove, eager for a meal.

Even in the gray darkness, Pedru could see how thin they were. They looked almost as if one skinny human arm was all they'd had to eat between them since the rains began. They were young and inexperienced, and so hungry that they were not at all wary. Pedru remembered how carefully Puna had crept down the hillside, alert to the slightest sound. Her sons were so different.

Samir, the larger of the two, went straight for the goat, reaching up and batting at it with his paws. Pedru knew that neither John nor Issa would risk a shot at him yet, in case it startled their more important target. But Anjani was still enough of a cub to be curious about anything new. The sound of the bush pig fascinated him. He searched at the foot of John's tree, scrambling in the dead leaves and bark to find the source of the noise, completely absorbed in what he was doing and completely unaware of any danger. And while he was at the foot of the tree, neither John nor Issa could get a clear shot.

But Pedru could.

Once again, just as on the evening that now seemed so long ago, when Pedru had lost his arm, time slowed to a stop and all the sound — the squealing, the crunch of paws in the leaf litter, even Pedru's own pounding heart — drained away.

The only things in all the world were Pedru and his lion.

Pedru stared down at the long pale back, streaked with shadows; the springy tail waving like a whip; the dark tufts of mane, much more numerous now than when they had first met; the notched left ear; the huge paws.

Pedru's arm was lifted, ready, his hand clasped

around his sharpened spear. He aimed at a point just behind the left shoulder. He estimated that at this distance he could pierce the animal's heart. It would be dead in moments. The lion who had stolen his arm was in his power at last. He could take his revenge on this hateful, wicked, evil beast, just as he had planned from the start. The lion had taken so much, so very, very much, of his life and of the lives of many others.

But the lion did not look hateful, or wicked. It merely looked like itself — no longer just "lion," but Anjani. Puna's son. The brother of Samir and little Cheli and Seti. A young hunter with a lot to learn, making his way in the world, making mistakes, growing up.

Pedru's arm fell limp by his side. Tears ran down his face.

Down below, Anjani found the little plastic speaker and crunched it in his teeth. Then he turned his attention to dinner.

Phht! Phht! The darts swished through the air

like hornets. In minutes, the two lions were stretched out, fast asleep in the Land Rover's headlights.

While the team got the collars on and took pictures of the lions, Pedru crouched by Anjani's head and ran his fingers through the knots of mane. He rubbed his finger on the scar, like a dark star on the lion's brow.

"You put that there," said Issa softly, coming to crouch beside him.

Pedru nodded.

"I saw you," Issa said, "in the tree, with your spear raised. It would have gone straight through his heart."

"Yes," said Pedru, "but a dead lion cannot give me back my arm. A dead lion can give nothing back. But a living lion . . ." Pedru looked up into his father's face. "I think Renaldo is right. There is so much a living lion could give us."

Issa put his hand on the top of Pedru's head. "You see? I told you," he said. "You did not need two arms to be strong."

Chapter Fourteen

Pedru was giving a talk to the whole school about lions. Renaldo was helping. He'd rigged up a big projector screen so that everyone could see the photographs of the lions. Pedru began with a picture of Puna and her four fluffy dandelion-yellow cubs. Some of the children simply couldn't believe that lions started life so small.

"Most cubs don't make it," Pedru told the children. "They starve to death or are killed by other predators, or by lions that take over their pride."

Pedru told the children about how lions work together to hunt their prey and live in big families. He told the children how clever and strong lions are. Then he showed them a picture of Anjani and Samir with their radio collars on, standing over a zebra that they had just killed.

"This one," Pedru said, pointing to the dark-maned lion, "is the lion who attacked me."

The children gasped.

"But because he wears a collar, we can tell where he is, so he can never sneak up on anyone again! Also," Pedru continued, "here are all the ways we keep safe from lions in our village."

Renaldo clicked on the next picture, and a big poster popped up. It showed people putting up fences to keep bush pigs and lions out of crops; it showed people sleeping outside in shelters on stilts so lions couldn't get them; it showed people walking at night with good, bright flashlights to frighten predators away. And it also showed people doing the exact opposite in a very funny way. The pictures made everyone laugh, and the children were all very pleased when Pedru told them that there was a copy of the poster for every child to take home.

After the talk, Mr. Mecula shook Pedru's hand.

"You are a talented artist, Pedru. Your pictures on the poster will show many, many people how to stay safe from lions."

"My left-handed writing's a bit better now, too!" said Pedru. "Thanks, Mr. Mecula. I'd never have found out I could draw if you hadn't given me that book."

"You'd never have found out you could draw if you still had your right hand, Pedru."

Outside in the school yard, John had been helping the younger children make animal masks from paper plates and rubber bands.

"I knew that art course I took in college would come in handy one day." He grinned.

Little zebras and waterbuck were being chased around by lions and leopards, although nobody had wanted to be a hyena. Zibi and Aji were running around hand in hand and roaring, even though Pedru told them that cheetahs didn't roar.

Beth and Issa were talking to the grown-ups, showing them the lion collars. Issa put earphones on Adalia, who almost jumped out of her skin when she heard the *bleep bleep bleep* signal coming from one of the collars that was inside the Land Rover.

"Oh, my goodness," said Adalia, laughing. "I thought a lion was right behind me!"

Mamma Ramina and Mamma Lago stood proudly behind a table, handing out rolled-up posters and homemade cookies to a long line of children.

Renaldo put his hand on Pedru's shoulder. "Well done. You did a great job," he said. "Now there's somebody I want you to meet."

The young man beside Renaldo took off his sunglasses and smiled. Pedru recognized him at once from his picture in the paper: Mauricio Kapango, the best forward the Black Mambas had ever had. Pedru couldn't speak. He just shook Mauricio's hand in wonder.

"I hear you're a lion expert, Pedru," Mauricio said. "I'm gonna need some lion experts when I build my safari lodge in Madune."

It wasn't long before the word spread that Mauricio Kapango, *the* Mauricio Kapango, was right there for real. Soon he was surrounded by a crowd of very excited children.

"So," he said, "shall we play a game? Do you have a ball?"

Everyone fell quiet.

"Well, yes," said Samuel, stepping forward. "But it's not really good enough." He held up the tangle of string and grass that they used for a ball.

Mauricio grinned. "This is like the ball I learned to shoot with. It'll be great to play with one again."

Pedru decided that it was the best, best, best day of his whole life. He scored the winning goal from Mauricio's pass, and then Enzi, Samuel, and all of his class carried him around the school on their shoulders.

As they put him down, Samuel said, "Good to have you back."

"Really, really good," said Enzi.

Pedru smiled. "I was thinking," he said. "It's been a while since we've gone fishing. . . ."

Epilogue

Pedru is listening to the *bleep bleep bleep* on his headphones that tells him where the lions are. He tunes in another frequency to locate the last radio collar and turns the antenna to pick up its direction. There! Now he knows where the visitors at the safari lodge should look tomorrow, to have the best chance of seeing lions. He'll call his father's cell phone and tell him. His father is the lodge's best guide, the one the foreign visitors all ask for. Adalia works at the lodge now, too. She says it's to pay for Aji and Zibi to go to college in Cape Town, like Pedru did. Issa says it's because she likes bossing people around.

Pedru looks out from the high hilltop as the sun begins to sink. From up here, he can see so much: the lovely loop of the river, the flat green valley and rocky highlands, and, down there, the village where he grew up. It looks much the same as when he was a boy. The houses still stand around a central space, where people meet and boys play soccer. But there are differences. There's a bathhouse in the middle of the village now, with water piped from a deep well. Everyone can drink and wash without risking an attack by the crocodiles down at the river! There's a school, too. And now that it's getting dark, lights come on. Not lanterns or candles, but bright electric lights — lights you can study and sew by. The lights are powered by the row of solar panels that Pedru helped to build on the south side of the village just two years ago. Lights pick out the thick thorn hedge that borders the marashambas, keeping bush pigs and the lions that follow them out of the crops. You can just see from here that each family's land now has a sturdy hut on stilts, so when people sleep out with their crops, they are safe.

It's time for Pedru to go. The bleeps have told him something, too: where the A Pride will be tonight. Pedru will spend the night watching them through his nightscope, recording their behavior for his PhD. It's not the biggest pride in his study area, but it is his favorite. *A* stands for Anjani, because Anjani and Samir were the pride's males for four years — a long time for lions to hold on to a pride. Anjani and his brother have been dead for a decade now, but Anjani's granddaughters are still the heart of the A Pride. They have taught Pedru so many things about how lions hunt and live and get around the problems that humans cause them.

As he climbs down from the hilltop, Pedru finds himself talking in his head to the lion, Anjani, just as he did as a boy. *Yes,* he tells him, *you stole my arm, but look at what you have given me in return.*

LIVING WITH LIONS

Hundreds of thousands of years ago, when humans still used stone tools and hunted for their food, lions were found in every part of the world except for Australia and Antarctica. Stone Age people made pictures of lions on rocks and cave walls. Ever since then, lions have been important to humans. There are lions in myths and stories, lions on TV and in movies. Everyone knows what a lion is. In fact, I bet that "lion" was one of the first animals that you could name when you were very little.

It's hard to imagine a world without lions, but that may be exactly what we're heading for. Today, most lions live in Africa, along with just a few hundred on one nature reserve in India. In the last ten years, the number of lions in Africa has dropped, so that there are only about 30,000 lions left there. That sounds like a lot, until you think that 30,000 is about the population of a medium-size town. Some scientists believe that lions could be extinct in the wild in ten years.

Why are lions in such danger? Well, the problem is that lions are not easy to live with. They are big, fierce predators, and they don't mind eating cows, goats, sheep, or even people. When there were fewer people and there was more wilderness for lions to live in, this didn't matter so much, as humans and lions could keep out of each other's way. But now the human population in East Africa, where most lions live, has grown so much that there's less wild food and wild space for lions. This means that more and more farm animals and people are being attacked — and even killed — by them. So you can understand why the people who have to live with lions are happy to shoot them, poison them, and let hunters from other countries pay money to kill them. This is exactly what is happening in Africa right now.

Luckily, groups of scientists and local people all over East Africa are working together to keep both people and lions safe.

Sometimes, this is just about changing the way people do things. The Niassa Carnivore Project in Mozambique found that lion attacks could be prevented by asking people to follow a few simple rules, like never sleeping in the open and always carrying a flashlight at night. They spread the word about this by using posters that even people who couldn't read would understand.

Niassa Carnivore Project Team

Good, strong fences really help, too. Fences around villages and crops keep lions' wild prey out, so that they have no reason to wander in after it and come face-to-face with a human. Putting domestic animals inside a barn or behind a fence at night keeps valuable cattle, sheep, and goats — which can be a family's lifeline — from ending up as a lion's dinner.

Knowing exactly where lions are can keep people and their animals from getting into danger. Putting satellite or radio tags on lions means they can be tracked over long distances, and if lions get close to villages or grazing cattle, people can be warned. The Living with Lions project in Kenya employs local Maasai warriors — who once hunted lions — as Lion Guardians. They use tracking equipment and cell phones to spread information about what lions are up to, they help to find lost cattle before lions do, and they keep a lookout for poachers — people who hunt and kill wild animals like lions and elephants illegally.

In many parts of Africa, lions struggle to find wild prey because the habitat where their prey lives has been taken over by farms, villages, or roads. In some places, humans kill and eat the same wild animals as lions. It's known as bush meat, and it's an important part of many Africans' diets. Without their natural wild prey to eat, lions turn to domestic animals and humans for their meals. But if the wild habitat is protected and people have domestic animals to eat, not wild ones, then there is more food for lions, and they aren't so eager to eat humans or farm animals.

Keeping humans and lions apart, tracking lions, and safeguarding their natural food all help people to live safely with lions. This makes people less likely to want to kill lions and more likely to see that they can be useful. Lions keep down the numbers of crop-munching animals, like bush pigs, which is important in Africa, where many families grow their own food. What's more, lions make money. Lots and lots of it.

Millions of tourists visit Africa every year to see big, exciting animals like lions. A single male lion brings about $500,000 worth of tourist money into its country in its lifetime, and Kenya's 2,000 lions bring $30 million into their country every year.

The problem is that the people who make money from lions, such as those in the hotel and airline industries, are not the people who have to pay for living with them. Keeping safe from lions by building fences, carrying flashlights, and using tags and cell phones costs money — money that people who live on farms and in villages simply don't have. For the people who have to live with lions, who sometimes lose their lives and loved ones to them, killing lions is the cheapest way to stay safe.

So what can we do to help save lions? One way is to make sure that some of that tourist money gets to the farmers and cattle herders who live with lions, so they can pay for fences, strong houses, lights, and all the other things that keep them safe from lion attacks. Another way is for people like you and me, all over the world, to give some of our money to the conservation projects that are working to help people live with lions, in hope and pride, not fear.